THE LIBRARY OF THE WESTERN HEMISPHERE™

Exploring BRAZIL

with the FIVE Themes of Geography

by Jane Holiday

The Rosen Publishing Group's
PowerKids Press™
New York

Published in 2005 by The Rosen Publishing Group, Inc.
29 East 21st Street, New York, NY 10010

First Edition

Editor: Geeta Sobha
Book Design: Michelle Innes

Photo Credits: Cover, p. 1 © Adrian Lyon/Getty Images; p. 9 © Royalty-Free/Corbis; p. 9 (Pantanal) © Steve Winter/National Geographic Image Collection; p. 10 © Roine Magnusson/Getty Images; p. 10 (turtle) © David A. Northcott/Corbis; p. 12 © David Katzenstein/Corbis; p. 12 (church) © Jeremy Horner/Corbis; p. 15 © James Davis, Eye Ubiquitous/Corbis; pp. 15 (orange grove), 19 © Stephanie Maze/Corbis; p. 15 (oranges) © Photodisc; pp. 16, 21 (Amazon) © Jacques Jangoux/Getty Images; p. 16 (Sao Paulo) © Larry Dale Gordon/Getty Images; p. 19 (train station) © Barnabas Bosshart/Corbis; p. 21 © Kevin Schafer/Getty Images

Library of Congress Cataloging-in-Publication Data

Holiday, Jane.
    Exploring Brazil with the five themes of geography / by Jane Holiday.— 1st ed.
    p. cm. — (The library of the Western Hemisphere)
    Includes index.
    ISBN 1-4042-2679-6 (lib. bdg.) — ISBN 0-8239-4639-8 (pbk.)
    1. Brazil—Geography—Juvenile literature. I. Title. II. Series.

F2510.9.H65 2005
918.1—dc22

2004005594

Manufactured in the United States of America

Contents

The FIVE Themes of Geography

Geography is the study of Earth, including its people, resources, climate, and physical features. To study a particular country or area, we use the five themes of geography: location, place, human-environment interaction, movement, and regions. These themes help us organize and understand important information about the geography of places around the world. Let's use the five themes to find out about the geography of Brazil.

1 Location

Where is Brazil?

To define where Brazil is you can use its absolute, or exact, location. Absolute location tells exactly where a place is in the world. The imaginary lines of longitude and latitude are used to give a place its absolute location.

Relative, or general, location is also used to show where a place is. Relative location describes where a place is in relation to other places near it. The cardinal directions of east, west, north, and south also define the relative location of a place.

2 Place

What is Brazil like?

To answer this question, we must study the physical and human features of Brazil. The physical features include landforms, natural resources, bodies of water, climate, and plant and animal life. The human features are things, such as cities, buildings, government, and traditions, that have been created by people.

3 Human-Environment Interaction

How do the people and the environment of Brazil affect each other?

Human-environment interaction explains how people rely on the environment. It also explains how people have adapted to, or changed to fit, the environment. Lastly, it explains how the environment affects the way people live.

4 Movement

How do people, goods, and ideas get from place to place in Brazil?

This theme explains how people, products, and ideas move around the country. It can also show how they move from Brazil to other places around the world.

5 Regions

What does Brazil have in common with other places around the world? What features do places within Brazil share to make them part of a region?

Places are grouped into regions by features that they share. This section looks at political and physical regions within Brazil. It also studies features that Brazil shares with other areas, making it part of a certain region.

Brazil's absolute location is 10° south and 55° west. Brazil's relative location is described by looking at the places that surround it. Brazil shares common borders with every South American country except Ecuador and Chile. To the north are Venezuela, Guyana, Suriname, and French Guiana. Paraguay, Bolivia, Peru, and Colombia are on Brazil's western border. Uruguay and Argentina are to the south of Brazil. To the east, Brazil is bordered by the Atlantic Ocean.

Where in the World?

Absolute location is the point where the lines of longitude and latitude meet.

Longitude tells a place's position in degrees east or west of the prime meridian, a line that runs through Greenwich, London.

Latitude tells a place's position in degrees north or south of the equator, the imaginary line that goes around the middle of the earth.

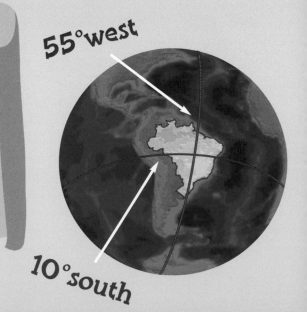

55°west

10°south

Brazil is the fifth-largest country in the world. Its capital is Brasília.

Physical Features

Brazil can be divided into five main geographical regions: North, Northeast, Southeast, South, and Center-West. The North covers almost half of the country. The Amazon River runs through this area. The Amazon rain forest covers mesas and mountains of the Guiana Highlands in the North.

In the Northeast are coastal plains and a large, dry area, which is known as the *sertão*. There are often droughts, or long spells of dry weather, in the *sertão*. The Center-West contains forest areas and the Pantanal, which is mostly made up of swamps and marshes. In the South, the country's smallest region, there are wide plains called pampas. The Southeast has lowlands, plains, hills, mountains, and a narrow coastal belt.

The Pantanal is one of the largest wetland areas in the world.

Iguaçu Falls lies on the border between Brazil and Argentina.

The yellow-headed sideneck, the world's largest freshwater turtle, lives in the Amazon rain forest.

The golden lion tamarin lives high in the rain forest of Brazil.

Most of Brazil gets warm temperatures that are over 72°F (22°C). The Amazon area gets about 90 inches (229 centimeters) of rain a year. In the South, temperatures in the mountains can get cool enough for snow.

Tapirs, pumas, sloths, and bush dogs are among the wildlife in Brazil. There are birds such as roadrunners, ibis, and herons. Many types of monkeys can be found in the Amazon rain forest. Dolphins, piranhas, and electric eels live in the waters. Reptiles include the fer-de-lance snake and the yellow-headed sideneck turtle.

The *cerrado* is land in central Brazil that has a mix of trees, shrubs, and grass. In the South, there is grassland called *campos*. Along the coast, there are mangrove trees. Many trees in the Amazon rain forest cannot be found elsewhere in the world. These include the Brazil nut tree and the cupuaça tree.

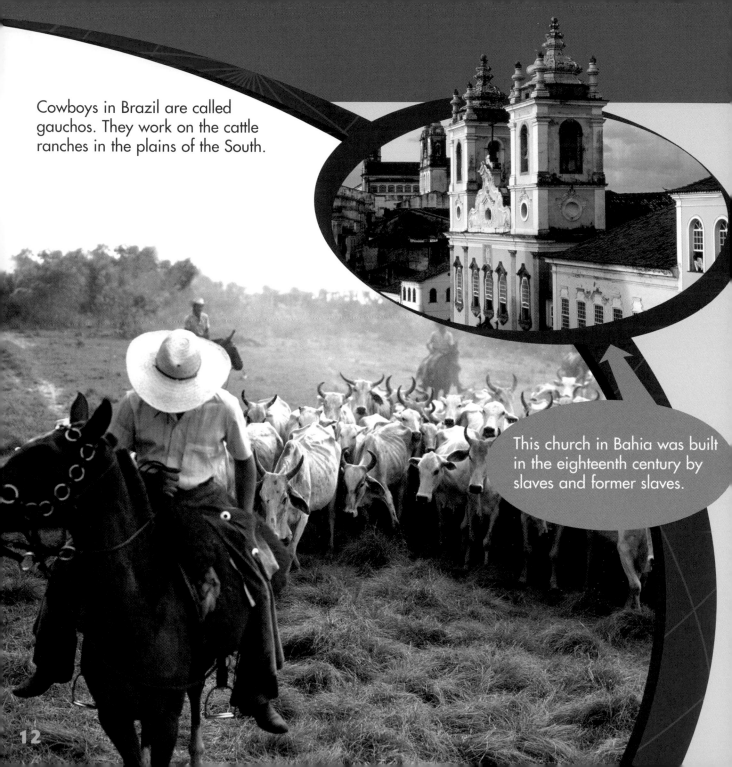

Cowboys in Brazil are called gauchos. They work on the cattle ranches in the plains of the South.

This church in Bahia was built in the eighteenth century by slaves and former slaves.

Human Features

Over 182,000,000 people live in Brazil. More than 80 percent of them live in and around the cities. The largest cities are São Paolo and Rio de Janeiro. Brazil is a federal republic. The president is elected by the people for a six-year term.

Most Brazilians are descended from Europeans, Native Americans, and African peoples. Brazil was a colony of Portugal. The official language of Brazil is Portuguese. Colonial architecture can still be seen in towns such as Ouro Preto. Modern buildings are found in cities such as Brasília and Rio de Janeiro.

Samba and *bumb-meu-boi* are styles of dances in Brazil. Bossa nova music was developed in Brazil. *Sertanejo* is a type of Brazilian country music. The most popular sport in Brazil is soccer.

Brazilians use their natural resources to meet their needs. Farmers grow fruits such as lemons, bananas, oranges, and mangoes. They also grow soybeans, rice, and cassava. Coffee and sugarcane are the largest crops grown in Brazil.

There are many mineral resources in the country. Brazil is the world's largest producer of iron ore. Gold, tin, and bauxite are also important mineral resources. Oil is found in the Northeast.

Many of Brazil's rivers are used to create hydroelectric power, which provides most of the country's electricity. Dams, such as Itaipú Dam, have been built in many parts of the country.

The rain forests provide many major resources. For example, trees are used for wood, plants are used to make medicine, and rubber is tapped from trees.

Brazil produces a third of the oranges used in the world.

The Itaipú Dam was built on the Paraná River at the border of Brazil and Paraguay. It is one of the largest hydroelectric power plants in the world.

São Paulo is the largest industrial city in South America.

Brazil's rain forest produces a great amount of oxygen. People are concerned that the loss of the rain forest will affect the entire world.

As Brazilians take advantage of their resources, often their actions affect their country's natural environment. The building of hydroelectric dams has flooded and destroyed animal habitats. Factories and automobiles are the main causes of pollution in urban areas, such as Rio de Janeiro and São Paulo. Also, mining can pollute water and destroy land.

The loss of rain forests has been a major issue in Brazil. In order to build the Trans-Amazonian Highway, many trees were cut down. Building farms has also contributed to loss of rain forest areas. When trees are cut down, many animals, such as the jaguar and many types of monkeys, lose their homes and may become extinct.

The Brazilian government has taken many steps to protect the land and wildlife. State parks, such as Jaú, as well as reserves have been set up across the country.

People and goods move about Brazil in many ways. Brazil has 1,071,821 miles (1,724,929 kilometers) of highways. A national highway system connects Brasília to all major cities. The Trans-Amazonian Highway goes up into the rain forest region.

Waterways are also important to movement in Brazil. Goods are shipped in and out of ports, such as Santos. Other important ports include Belém, Rio de Janeiro, and Paranaguá.

Brazil has 665 airports. Every large city has an airport. Small airports allow travel to the hard-to-reach areas in the Amazon region.

Brazilians get information in many ways. Over 300 newspapers are published daily in Brazil, including *O Estado de São Paulo* and *Jornal do Brasil*. There are over 200 television stations and over 2,500 radio stations.

Trains move people to and from the cities of Rio de Janeiro, São Paulo, and Brasília.

Santos is the world's largest coffee-shipping port.

Brazil is part of both physical and cultural regions. It belongs to the cultural region known as Latin America. The people of Latin America speak a Romance language, such as Portuguese, Spanish, or French. Latin America is made up of countries in the Western Hemisphere, south of the United States, including the West Indies.

Brazil falls within the physical region of South America. The country itself is divided into the physical regions of the Guiana Highlands, the Amazon Lowlands, Pantanal, the Brazilian Highlands, and the Coastal Lowlands.

Brazil is divided into 26 states. Each state has its own government. Brazil also has one federal district, its capital, Brasília.

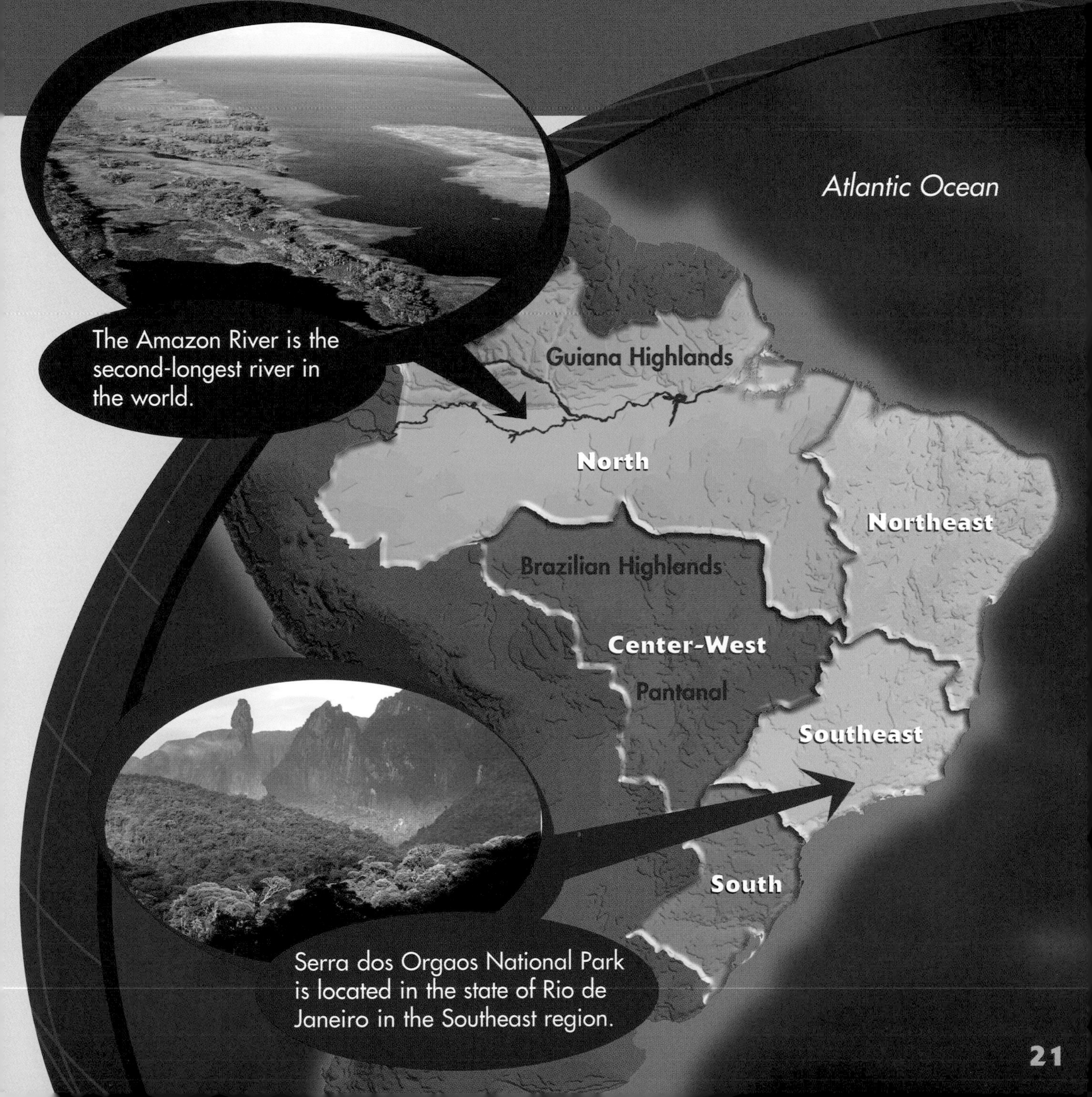

The Amazon River is the second-longest river in the world.

Atlantic Ocean

Guiana Highlands

North

Northeast

Brazilian Highlands

Center-West

Pantanal

Southeast

Serra dos Orgaos National Park is located in the state of Rio de Janeiro in the Southeast region.

South

Brazil's Flag

Population (2003) 182,032,600

Language Portuguese

Absolute location 10° south, 55° west

Capital city Brasília

Area 3,300,171 square miles (8,547,404 square kilometers)

Highest point Pico da Neblina 9,888 feet (3,014 meters)

Lowest point Atlantic Ocean zero feet

Land boundaries Argentina, Bolivia, Colombia, French Guiana, Guyana, Paraguay, Peru, Suriname, Uruguay, and Venezuela

Natural resources iron ore, manganese, bauxite, nickel, uranium, phosphates, tin, gold, platinum, petroleum, and timber

Agricultural products soybeans, coffee, tobacco, sugarcane, cacao beans, beef, and poultry

Major exports road vehicles and parts, coffee and coffee substitutes, metals, soybeans, and footwear

Major imports machinery, chemical products, and oil

Glossary

architecture (AR-ki-tek-chur) The style in which buildings are designed.

descended (di-SEND-ud) To belong to a later generation of the same family.

extinct (ek-STINGKT) No longer existing.

habitat (HAB-uh-tat) The place where animals or plants live.

hydroelectric power (hye-droh-i-LEK-trik POU-ur) Water power that is used to turn a generator to produce electricity.

interaction (in-tur-AK-shuhn) The action between people, groups, or things.

marsh (MARSH) An area of wet, low land.

mesa (MAY-suh) A hill or mountain with steep sides and a flat top.

region (REE-juhn) An area or a district.

resource (ri-SORSS) Something that is valuable or useful to a place or person.

urban (UR-buhn) To do with or living in a city.

Index

A
Amazon Lowlands, 20
Amazon rain forest, 8,
  11
Amazon River, 8
Atlantic Ocean, 6

B
Brasília, 13, 18, 20
Brazilian Highlands, 20

C
Coastal Lowlands, 20
colonial architecture, 13
crops, 14

D
dams, 14, 17
dance, 13

E
environment, 5, 17

F
farmers, 14
federal republic, 13

G
Guiana Highlands, 8, 20

H
habitats, 17
hydroelectric power, 14

I
Itaipú Dam, 14

L
Latin America, 20

M
mangrove trees, 11
music, 13

P
pampas, 8
Pantanal, 8, 20

pollution, 17
ports, 18

R
region, 4, 5, 8, 20
resources, 4, 5, 14
Rio de Janeiro, 13, 17,
  18
rivers, 14

S
São Paolo, 13, 17
sertão, 8
soccer, 13

T
Trans-Amazonian
  Highway, 17, 18

W
waterways, 18
wildlife, 11, 17

Web Sites

Due to the changing nature of Internet links, PowerKids Press has developed an on-line list of Web sites related to the subject of this book. This site is updated regularly. Please use this link to access the list:
http://www.powerkidslinks.com/lwh/brazil